YOU ARE INVITED

B⁺day y

WHO: GRANDMA
WHEN: OCTOBER 24, 2016
WHERE: 257 CAPLAN AVE

For Kyle.
Be patient. We have
all the time in the world.

Bethany & David

This book was edited by Bethany Strout and designed by David Caplan.

First published in Great Britain in 2016 by Andersen Press Ltd.,
20 Vauxhall Bridge Road, London SWIV 2SA.

Originally published by Little, Brown and Company, Hachette Book Group, 1290
Avenue of the Americas, New York, NY 10104, USA.

Copyright © Dan Santat, 2016.

The rights of Dan Santat to be identified as the author and illustrator of this work
have been asserted by him in accordance with the
Copyrights, Designs and Patents Act, 1988.

Printed and bound in China.

10 9 8 7 6 5 4 3 2 1

British Library Cataloguing in Publication Data available.

ISBN 978 1 78344 467 0 (hardback)

ISBN 978 1 78344 516 5 (paperback)

This book belongs to:

....

The car trip to visit Grandma is always exciting!

But after the first hour,

it can feel like an eternity.

You might find yourself saying things like,

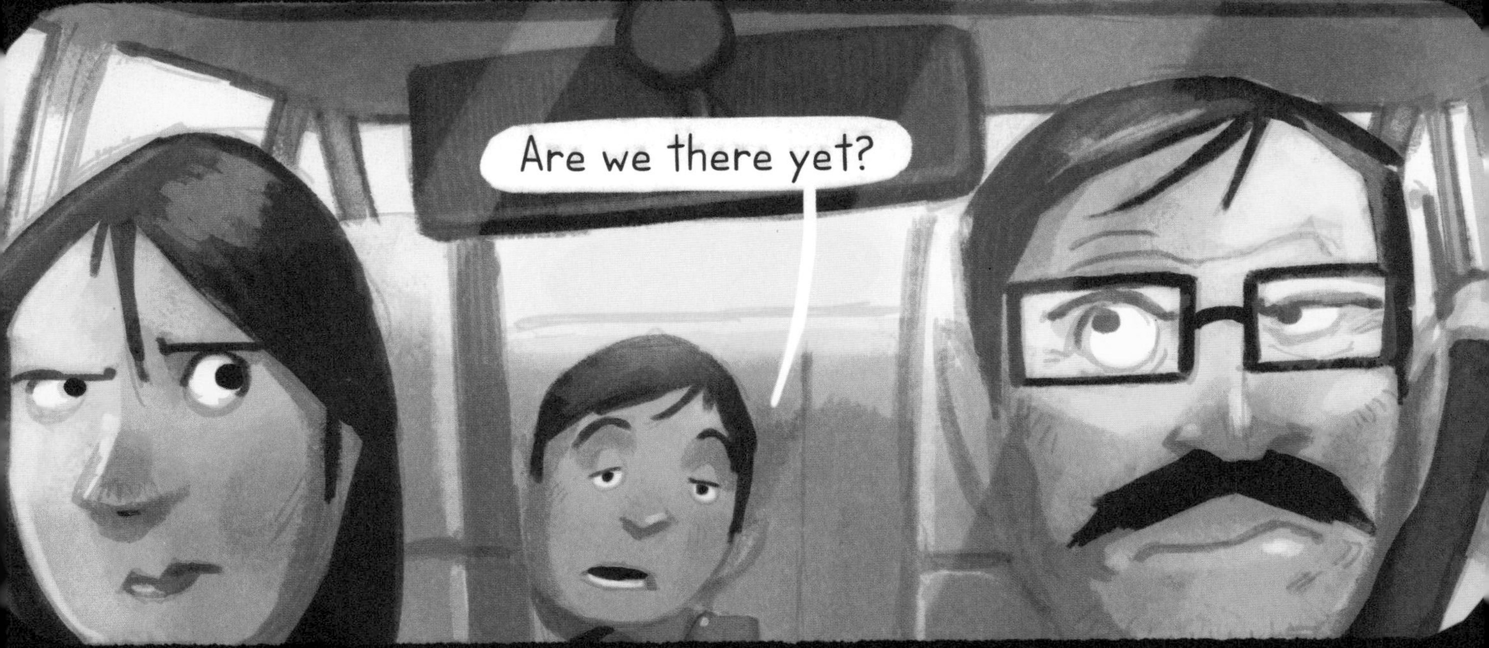

or,

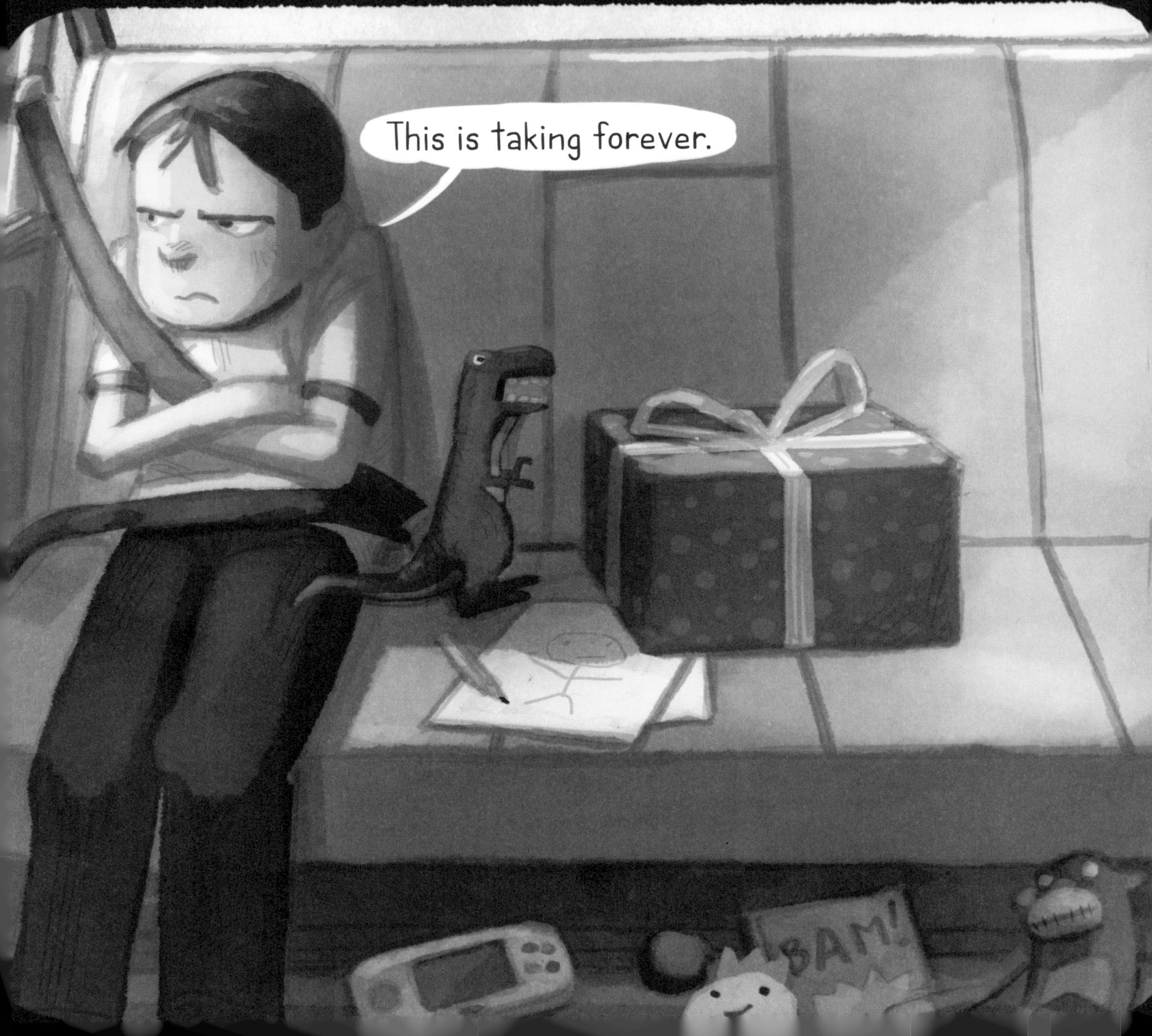

Staring out your window at a thousand miles of road can get boring pretty quickly. Not even all the toys in the world can help.

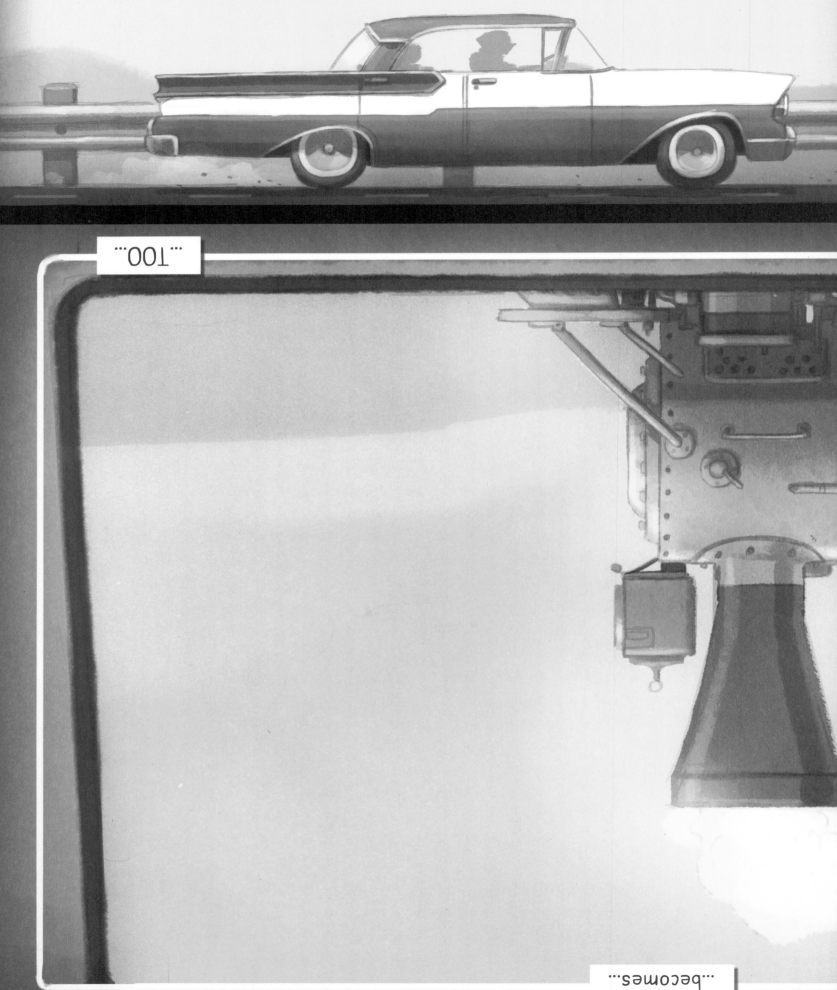

...100...

...becomes...

But what happens when your brain  bored?

Minutes begin to feel like hours.

...but it feels like it's been a million years.

WELCOME.

DISTR

CAPLAN AVE

YIELD   CAUTION

NO
DROP
ZONE

TAKEOFF

ONE WAY

NO
PARKING

GRILL
SINCE 1979

The road is full of twists and turns...

And you...   ...never...   ...know...

...where...   ...life...   ...may...

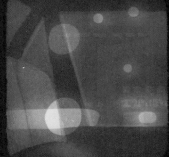

...take...   ...you.

So sit back and enjoy the ride.

But remember, there's no greater gift than the present.

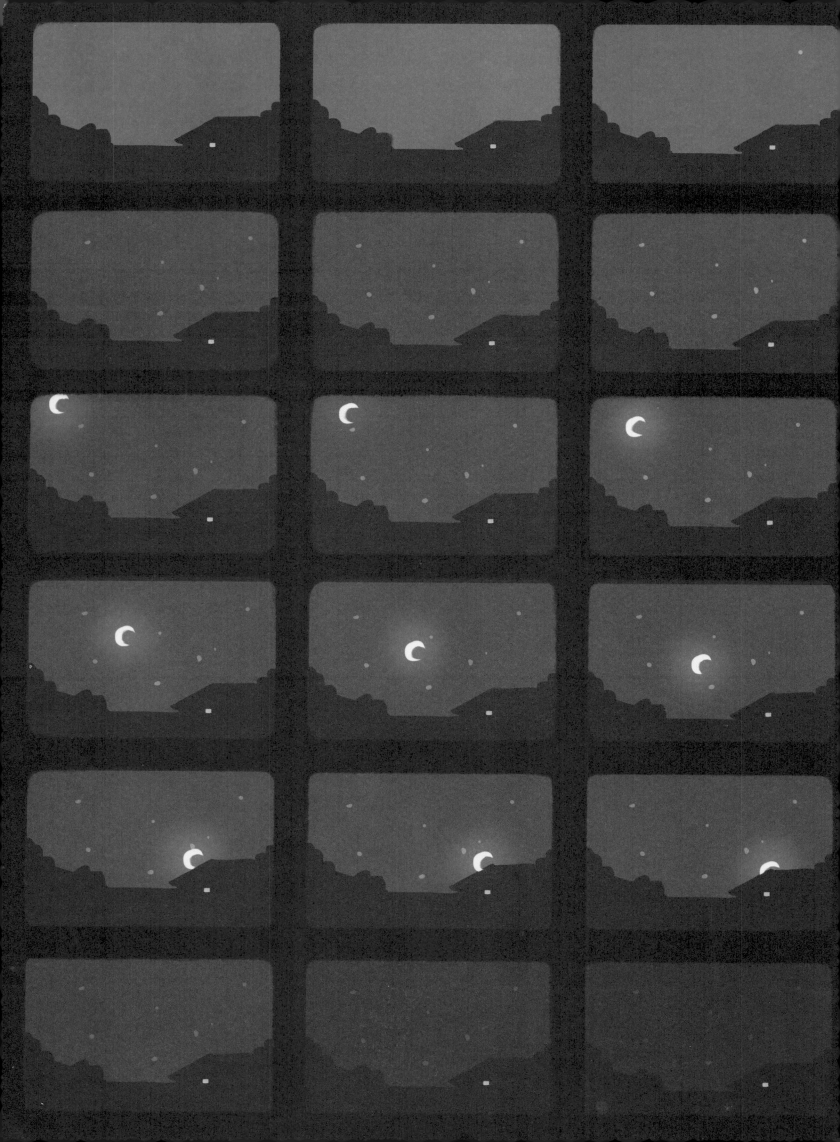

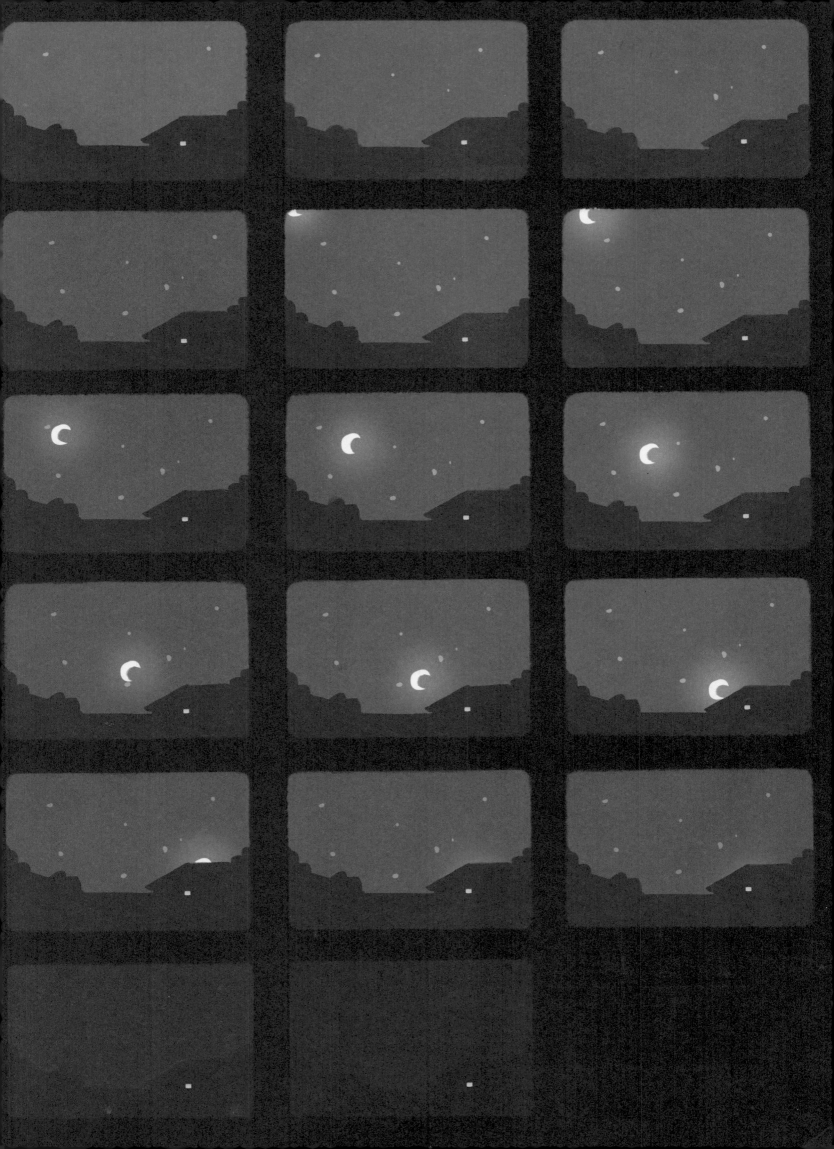